YUCKY, 3
DISGUSTINGLY
GROSS. ICKY
short STORIES

YUCKY, DISGUSTINGLY GROSS, ICKY short STORIES **3**

BUTT BLAST

SUSAN BERRAN

FOR YOUNG READERS

For Mel & Andrena.
For being there every step of the way.

Contents

THE "HAIR FAIRIES"

Part One

Geez life sucks! It's **sOOO** unfair!

I came home from school after a totally awesome day. I broke Jared's record for landing the most dead blow-flies on Crabby Abbey's head during math class—which, by the way, is now twenty-three—using our awesome, one-of-a-kind, *fantasmagorical* invention, the "single shot bug flinger." But before I could even throw my schoolbag on the floor and grab a snack from the kitchen, Mom came

stomping out of the bathroom and scared the absolute crap out of me!

She looked like some weird zombie, wearing one of those "germ protection oxygen suits" like the ones they wear in lame, old horror movies. You know, those really dumb ones where some dimwit goes to the jungle to help save the monkeys. Dimwit gets scratched by a monkey. The monkey turns out to be sick. The sick monkey dies. The dimwit gets sick, so he hops on a plane and flies back home. He coughs all over everyone in the plane. The plane lands and the passengers sneeze all over everyone at the airport. The people at the airport jump on more planes and cough over more people, who cough over everyone at home, who sneeze over everyone at work, who

spit-up all over their customers, and *ta dah*, the whole world is suddenly bleeding from the eyes with brains exploding all over the place and *blah blah blah blah blah*.

Ok, so what was I writing about . . . oh yeah, I know.

So Mom came out of the bathroom looking like someone had smooshed together Darth Vader and a surgeon from outer space. Her head was completely covered with a black shower cap, and messy, wiry bits of hair poked out all over the place. Another black mask covered the bottom half of her face, leaving just her eyes peeping out over the top.

She was wearing long, pink rubber gloves that reached her elbows and the kitchen apron that I got her for Christmas—the one

with a picture of a zombie on it that said *"Eat More Brains!"* And to complete the "escaped mental patient" look she was obviously going for, underneath the apron, Mom was wearing oversized, black sweatpants and an old black top that was at least four sizes too big.

So "Doctor Darth Weirdo"—my Mom—
started slowly stomping towards me, and all
I could see was her unblinking, bloodshot
eyes. The sound of her deep, slow breathing
was escaping from underneath her mask.
Hhhhh hhhhh hhhhh. It was freaky.
Staring straight ahead with her arms outstretched towards me, I was looking for a
monkey bite on her body and waiting for her
to say ***"braaaiiins."*** I kicked my schoolbag against the wall and steeled myself as she
was obviously about to give me the hug from
hell.

Usually after school, Mom greeted me
by yelling, "Have you got any homework?
You're doing your homework before Jared
comes over! Don't tell me you haven't got any

8

homework! Everyone else gets homework!" But now she was only two steps away with her arms still stretched out and there was no yelling. Something very weird was obviously going on.

I took a few short, sharp breaths preparing myself for her incoming humongous hug. Then, as Mom zeroed in on me, I took one final enormous breath before I was completely smothered by her boobs. I knew I couldn't win. Even if I did escape her suffocating hug, there was a worse fate awaiting me—the "sweaty hairy-pit hug." I definitely did not want to breathe in any of Mom's soggy armpit sweat! It was absolutely deadly!

I learned my lesson when I nearly *died* last Christmas from Grandma's sweaty hairy-pit

hug. The memory was terrifying. Just like Mom, Grandma targeted me for the deadly "crusher cuddle"—her special one that she liked to give without her teeth in! *Eww-www!* Why couldn't she just kiss me on the cheek like normal people do? At least I could use the cheese grater afterwards to rip my cheek off and grow a new one. But *nooooo* I was just standing against the wall, minding my own business, when Grandma comes towards me ready for a hug. With her arms reaching forward it looked as if she had a massive bed sheet hanging from each arm, flapping about in the breeze. The skin-colored "sheets" were actually years and years of stretched, flabby skin. They swayed rhythmically from side to side, almost send-

ing me into a trance. With all that dangly skin I thought Grandma could jump out of a plane, hold her hands above her head, and *pop,* she'd have her own built-in parachute. She could be stranded on a desert island, build a raft, and travel back home using her arm flab as a sail.

So there I was, trapped with Grandma moving towards me as if she was herding cows and using her arms to create two brick walls. There was no way to escape. No way to make a run for it. No way to survive the hug of doom! Grandma took a final step toward me and then, like some mechanical terminator, her arms began to clamp around my shoulders and squeeze together to smother me!

Her face was moving towards mine—lips puckering and spit flying everywhere, because she had no teeth to keep the saliva in her mouth. Her arm flab was flapping, and without thinking I took a deep breath, bent my knees, and ducked to try and slip beneath the flab and her arm-lock. But obviously, all Grandmas know this escape move and won't give up their "hugs and kisses" that easily! She quickly turned her body to the side and shoved her leg across to block off my escape path and slipped her arms over my shoulders until they were locked on tightly around the very top of my head. With her arm flab acting as iron curtains, blinding and suffocating me all at the same time, my head was being squeezed like a giant upside-down pimple

until it suddenly *popped* out from beneath Grandma's clenched arms. I desperately sucked in another breath of air as I was buried face-first under Grandma's sweaty, soggy, warm armpit! Grandma got her hug all right. But now I have nightmares and totally freak out whenever a hair touches my face. *Eeewwwww!*

Now where was I? That's right. My Darth Vader look-a-like Mom came racing towards me with her arms outstretched. There was about seven seconds till "death by hug." I started taking deep, quick breaths. Six, five, four, three, two, one . . . here it comes. I froze waiting for Mom's hands to clamp me. But then she stopped dead, right in front of me, and instead of her arms clutching around my shoulders, she raised them like a human forklift and stuck both hands straight into my hair! Then she started digging about with her fingers, as if she was searching for long-lost buried treasure. And in her deep, raspy, mask-covered voice she shouted, "Ok Mister, straight into the bathroom. I have to treat you for nits!"

Nooooooooooooo!

PART TWO

I was so annoyed and totally peeved. Why did I have to get "treated"? The nits were in little Miss Smelly Poopy-Pants Melly's hair, not mine! But no. Mom said that we all would have to wash our hair with the special "nit-killer shampoo." Awesome!

My first day at daycare, I brought home a finger painting. Melly's first day at daycare and she brought home nits!

So now all three of us had to have this disgusting, gross, bright blue "lotion" smothered through our hair. Then it had to be completely covered with a shower cap before we sat around bored stiff for a couple of hours while it soaked through our hair, into our skull, and all the way into our brain. The smell was absolutely, positively disgusting!

It's like the worst smell in the entire universe! I reckon if we were ever invaded by space aliens, we would just have to shoot them with nit shampoo and that would stop them in their tracks!

Then Mom got even stranger than her Doctor Darth Zombie dress-up. She started getting all nervous and worried because she didn't want little Miss Melly Pong-Pants going to daycare the next day and running around singing, "Yay, I've got *ni-its*, I've got *ni-its*," and then all the kids going home and asking, "Can I have nits too, please Mommy? Melly has nits. *Pleeease* can I get some nits?" Mom was totally freaking out that *she'd* get the blame for *all* the other kids at daycare getting nits! For the rest of the afternoon,

Mom made me talk in her "secret nit code" so that little Miss Smelly wouldn't understand.

Great. So Mom, Melly, and I all had to sit in the bathroom wearing shower caps for ***three hours*** smelling like . . . like . . . oh I know, ear medicine mixed with Grandma's toilet cleaner! And talking about "hair fairies." Yep, you heard me—hair fairies! And of course, we had to have our little white dog, Fluff Butt, in there as well, to keep Melly happy. That's fair—not! Did Mom ask me if I'd like a sabre-toothed tiger to keep me happy? ***Nooo!***

Oh, and because I was the last one home, I had to wear the only shower cap that was left. The one that Mom had used to soak Fluff Butt's big, hairy butt in when she had butt

blisters—these really big, red, pussy blisters all over her backside from scraping it along the worn-out carpet whenever it was itchy, leaving long, gross skidmarks across the carpet. Mom was pretty cranky with Fluff Butt. The vet gave Mom this liquid to soak her butt in— the dog's butt, not Mom's!

Mom filled the shower cap with the dog's butt medicine and then pulled it over Fluff's backside and threw an elastic strap around it to hold it over her fluffy bottom. The boils then soaked in the liquid until they burst. So I knew the shower cap had been full of this gross, green, pussy butt-liquid. Mom said she cleaned the shower cap really well, but about a week later it was growing a garden of mold in it. *Eewwwww!*

19

"Lucky I didn't throw that shower cap out," Mom said, happy with herself. "Otherwise we wouldn't have had enough." Yeah sure, I felt *very* lucky to be wearing *that* on my head—not!

Meanwhile, little Miss Bulging-Butt Melly was wearing a cute, bright yellow "duck" shower cap. Actually, *my* bright yellow duck shower cap!

Little Miss Yelly Melly Itchy-Head was wearing *my* duck shower cap! She was wearing *my* duck shower cap that *I* got for *my* birthday when I was two! Melly was wearing *my* duck shower cap without anyone asking *me!*

Not that I cared . . . I didn't even wear the stupid baby shower cap anymore! Well,

maybe just when I'm trying not to get my hair wet . . . or in a hurry . . . or having a bath . . . or going for a swim . . . or having a shower. Hey, it's my ducky shower cap and I'll wear it whenever I want!!

Please don't tell anyone.

I was so annoyed! "Why do I have to use the stupid nit, I mean 'hair fairy,' shampoo? I haven't even got hair fairies!" I whined.

"Because!" Mom shouted with laser beam daggers shooting from her sharp, squinty eyes. "Because the hair fairies like to play in the long grass fields on the mountain and send little 'gifts' by airmail for everyone else and their mountain, whenever the mountains are close together."

"What??" I said staring blankly at Mom as

Melly sat in the bathtub splashing about—still with *my* ducky shower cap on.

"You know . . . and they love to send lots of their family and friends to new mountains to set up their new homes and build towns and cities," Mom hissed through gritted teeth.

What the heck was she talking about?!

"And now we're having a very special surprise party to farewell the hair fairies so that they can go and visit some where else far, far away."

"What?! I just wanna know why I can't go to Jared's . . . Melly's the one who has a zillion nits, not me!"

"I've got *ni-its*! I've got ni-its! I've got *ni-its*!" little Miss Poopy-Pants Melly began singing loudly and proudly.

Boy was Mom super cranky with me!

"What did I do?!" I asked innocently.

Well, it wasn't much of a secret code anyway. Geez!

Mom said that she'd explained the secret code we were meant to be using but I was so busy texting Jared that I obviously wasn't paying attention!

"Ah ha! So you admit it!" I said to Mom, obviously having caught her out. "You saw that I was texting Jared when you told me about the code! You knew I wasn't listening! It *was* actually your fault, not mine!"

Mom didn't agree! She took my phone off me and now I had to sit there, *without* a phone, in the bathroom listening to little Miss Snot Nose singing "I've got ni-its! I've got ni-its! I love my nits!" while Mom desperately tried to convince her that they were secret hair fairies.

I decided that if I wanted my phone back within the next ten years, I better start doing some emergency "Mom sucking-up." So while Melly was splashing about in the bath, Mom took off Melly's (my!) shower cap and began combing the tiny insects from her hair and rubbing them off onto a tissue. I said I would help by making sure they were totally squished dead.

Actually, that did start to make the afternoon sort of fun.

You see, nits are anywhere from the size of a pinhead to the size of a big ant. They are tough little bugs with a sort of see-through

abdomen. The only way you can be sure that they're dead is to cut them in half or "pop" them like a pimple! Awesome!

So while Melly splashed and sang, Mom combed and wiped them onto the tissue and I had to take my thumbnail and use it like a giant guillotine. I sliced straight down through the center of each nit! It was excellent! I used a magnifying glass to watch and man did those things squirt! Teeny, tiny guts were sent spraying in every direction. Onto the mirror, across the sink, and into Mom's open face cream. I wonder if Mom will notice that her cream is oilier and has legs when she smothers it all over her face before bed?

Occasionally I got bored watching guts spray all over the place so I'd "pop" them

instead. Their little nit-heads would fly across the room in all directions. One of the teeny, weeny little heads ricocheted across the room, off the door handle, up to the lightbulb, off the tap, and straight into Fluff Butt's food bowl. Fluff was eating at the time and sucked it up deep into his nostril. I think the little nit-head was still alive and used his teeth to grab hold of a nostril hair to save himself from going down the dog's throat, because Fluff started snorting and sneezing. Suddenly, he did this really weird snuffle, scrunched up his nose, and . . . *arrr arrr arrchoooo!* Melly was still singing when Fluff Butt sneezed and the nit-head flew back out of his nostril, ricocheted off the tap, up to the light, off the door

handle, across the room, and landed in Melly's mouth.

Awesome! My day just got a whole lot better.

So I guess nits, I mean "hair fairies," are good for something.

Does My Butt Smell?

I just don't get it! I'm innocently sitting around, minding my own business, when Mom suddenly appears in the living room doorway, casually wanders past me, and says ...
"Your butt smells!"

Huh? **What the?** And she wasn't kidding either. She was positively, absamativalutely serious! I totally did **not** know that!

For some strange, weird, Mom reason, she decides to tell me this incredibly interesting, and educational information right in the middle of my favorite television show! Surely such an important fact deserved more explanation than that?!

You see, up until then I'd always thought that your eyes "see," your hands "feel," your mouth "speaks," your ears "listen," and your *nose "smells"*!

I know that, you know that, everyone knows that! Or so I thought.

I just assumed that smell enters through the nostrils, slides upward, slips into your

skull, and slithers around the outside of your brain until it figures out what kind of smell it is. Whether it's so disgustingly gross that last night's dinner starts gurgling back up your throat, ready to spew out everywhere, or not.

But obviously, I'm wrong, you're wrong, we're all wrong! Because Mom decides to tell me the truth for the very first time in my entire life!

That's right, apparently my butt *smells* . . .

Why hasn't anyone ever told me this before? All my life I figured that whenever I smelled my little sister's gross, overflowing, poopy diapers, or the dog's massive, gut-chucking farts, the teacher's moldy cheese and garlic B.O. stench, that I was smelling them all through the nostrils on my **nose**. Now I find out, according to Mom, I am **actually** smelling everything through **my butt!**

That's incredible!

Hey, I wonder if it makes any difference what I'm wearing? Like if I'm wearing jeans or pants, will I be able to smell stuff as well as when I'm wearing loose shorts or sweatpants? Maybe I should be wearing boxers instead of my tight briefs to make sure I can smell better?

I'm betting that babies can hardly smell anything at all for the first few years of their life. Wearing those really thick diapers on their teeny, tiny pink backsides would be like wearing a big, thick, fluffy nose-plug on your butt!

32

Just as I sat pondering what to do with this new information, Mom wandered back into the room. She strolled past me again and casually said for the second time, "Your butt **really does** smell." She gave a quick grimace in my direction as she said it.

"I know! You've already told me!" I shot back, annoyed. Hey, I'm not deaf! I don't need to be told the same thing over and over. Unless, of course, my butt can hear as well? *Nahhhhh!*

My head suddenly flooded with a zillion and one questions. Mom's new little piece of information made me start to wonder about all sorts of stuff like . . . well, if everyone's butt does the smelling, then what the heck is the nose on the front of our head being used for?

It couldn't be stuck smack bang in the middle of peoples' faces just to make them look pretty. Because I've sure seen some really weird looking noses that definitely **do not** make the person look any better!

Some people get round ones. Others get wide ones. Some are thin and long. Some are like a slide, and others look like the big fat backside of an overweight orangutan. There are heaps of shapes and sizes. I reckon nature gives everyone a different nose for no reason at all!

But then again . . . maybe your nose *is* useful. I guess it could have something to do with your balance. It could be like the keel under a yacht that keeps it upright in the water, or the fin underneath a surfboard that keeps it steady.

If you think about it, when you were born you couldn't walk at all. You're a useless, little pink lump that lies about until someone picks you up off the floor. Your nose is a tiny little bump on your face—it's more like a pimple really. But as you start to grow, your nose starts to grow as well. Until one day, ***bammm,*** your nose is spread across half your face and suddenly you're learning to stand, walk, run, jump—amazing!

And when people with a cold get a blocked nose, they can barely get out of bed and walk around. They spend all day lying around until their nose is clear again.

It seems that the moment your nose gets blocked up, or isn't working properly, you totally lose your balance! So your nose really could be a sort of "human sail" to stop you falling over. And obviously the worse your balance is, the bigger your nose. That's why some people have a humongous, gigantasuarus nose that looks like Mount Everest.

Maybe we have a big nose in the middle of our face to take the attention away from other bits of our body that we want to draw attention away from.

Kind of like my neighbor. Her grandkids call her "Stinky Gran" because she always smells like the body odor of a dead sloth. She has the biggest, most gigantic, "butt"-shaped nose that I've ever seen! It covers her face so it looks like she has a huge nose stuck on top of her neck, with tiny eyes hiding behind it.

I don't think I've ever seen her whole face because it's camouflaged so well by her nose.

Yep, I think some people really need a big nose to hide behind.

So while our butts are smelling, our noses are keeping us standing upright and hiding all those really gross features that we don't want anyone to see.

Now that Mom has told me my butt smells, I definitely wanted to find out just **how** my butt smells stuff. And I couldn't wait to start testing some of my ideas.

I figured that my butt had to be an especially super-sensitive sniffer, because most of the time I'm sitting down. My butt must be able to smell through my pants, my undies, or even the couch, bed, chair, or anything else that I'm sitting on. Which could also mean that a lot of stuff smells different when I'm sitting down.

Like last night when I was lying on the couch, starving to death while Mom was cooking dinner, I took a whiff and it smelled like a truckload of really bad farts mixed with dead fish wrapped in dirty socks! But that could have been because I'd just let go a massive, ripper fart and my butt mixed the smell with Mom's dinner—and she really was cooking disgusting, dead fish in weird sauce!

I started thinking there are probably heaps of other smells that I totally miss out on when I'm lying around on the couch and not paying much attention.

I headed into my bedroom to start trying to figure out a bunch of smell tests that I could do to find out just how well my butt smells. That's when I realized that I'd actually already done the first test a couple of days ago when we went out to my Auntie and Uncle's goat farm for a barbecue lunch. It was a stinking hot day but luckily they have this awesome swimming pool. So, while Mom and Auntie Ree cooked lunch, I went for a swim with Uncle Karl.

I distinctly remember smelling sausages, steak, mushrooms, and onion cooking on the grill while my butt was **underwater** in the pool! So that means my butt must be the most awesome, super-sniffer **ever!**

I started to wonder if everyone else's butt can smell while underwater?

You should definitely try it out!
Next time you're in a pool, stand up so that your butt is still underwater.

Then suck in a huuuuge whiff with your butt...
if you can smell stuff, then you have a "Super Sniffer Butt" as well!

I was thinking about testing my theory out a bit further by swimming with a snorkel,

41

a hose, a bucket, and a can of baked beans. Before I got too far, Mom screamed out from the kitchen. ***"Get to the table for dinner!"***

As I headed towards the dinner table, I began preparing for my second experiment. I started clenching, unclenching, clenching, and unclenching my butt cheeks as tightly as possible to suck in all the smells of dinner. *Sniff, sniff, **sniff, sniff**. Ewwwww!* I didn't need to suck the smells into my butt very hard to know what ***that*** revolting aroma was. The stench floating out from the kitchen was from the grossest vegetable on earth! The totally unmistakable, "chuck-up" smell of sweaty armpits and burnt tires—brussel sprouts! Yeah, my butt could smell that green crap a mile away!

As I continued along the hallway towards the dinner table my head was churning—bursting with more ideas. It looked like I had the perfect opportunity to carry out another experiment and discover just how well my butt really could smell.

I turned around and started walking backwards to make sure that I didn't **see** what else was for dinner. Then as I stopped and stood backwards in the kitchen doorway, I clenched my butt cheeks as tightly as possible while I listened for Mom placing our plates on the table. But just as I heard Mom and my baby sister, Little Miss Smelly Melly Prissy-Pants, sit down in front of their steaming hot plate of, *umMM*, "food" Mom said, *"Guess what's for dinner?"* So I yanked down my pants, bent over, and pointed my big butt cheeks at the two of them, trying to suck in as many of the smells hanging in the air as possible. There was brussel sprouts, and *hmmmM*, something that smelled like some gross type of dead meat, and . . .

"Eewwwww. Bottom!" my snotty little sister squealed at the top of her voice.

"Sam!" Mom bellowed as she turned to follow Melly's gaze. "Pull up your pants!"

"But I'm experimenting!" I explained.

"I'll experiment with how long you can live without your Xbox if you don't pull your pants up right now!" Mom snapped.

"But I'm trying to figure out how my butt smells!" I tried to defend myself, while still shining my bare butt in their direction.

Then, for some weird reason Mom thought I was trying to be a "smart-butt" and told me to go to bed *without* dinner. Which is so not fair! After all, she was the one that told me my butt smells in the first place!

Sitting in my room, I figured I may as well do a few more experiments to help pass the time. I opened the window, hopped up onto my desk, yanked down my pants, and shoved my bare butt out the window; poking it outside into the cold evening breeze. I wanted to see what flowers and cars and other stuff I could smell.

But then for some odd reason, our neighbor came over, banged on our front door, and whined to Mom about my butt hanging out the window "for the whole world to see" and

I got into even **more** trouble with Mom!

Which totally sucked!

But I've been thinking, and I now know why I nearly choke to death from the smell in the toilet after eating curry. It's **way** too close to my sniffer.

Oh, and I've learned something else really cool too.

The other day at school my teacher called me a smart-butt and said she didn't know what was in my head. Then this morning, Mom said there was nothing between my ears. Wow! So now people are telling me that my skull is actually completely empty and it's my **butt** that's smart! Looks like I'll have to think of a new bunch of experiments to figure out why I have a big, empty head and whether it's both butt-cheeks that are smart or just one.

Awesome!

MAKING CANDLES FROM EAR WAX?

Part One

49

Can you make candles using earwax?

I don't know! I wouldn't have a clue! If you thought I was going to answer the question for you . . . well, big surprise! *I'm not!*

But, my best friend, Jared, and I did start digging out and collecting our own earwax ages ago. We kind of figured that earwax must be good for something! We just haven't found out what yet!

We've been experimenting to try and find out if earwax is just stale, old yellow boogers or not. We think that everyone probably starts off with a clear liquid, called saliva, in their guts. But when you get the sniffles, your spit is sucked up past the back of your mouth and straight up into your nose. And that's where it sits, hiding and slowly turning greeny-yellow.

It then starts getting thicker, moldier, and slimier as it begins turning into awesome, gross boogers. Then when your nose is absolutely chockers full, **bammm!** your snot can be shot out of your nose at a hundred miles an hour. A massive cannon-blast, flying across the room, landing on your friend's face or anything else that gets in its path.

So while some boogers get saved up in your nostrils and dug out later for a tasty snack, others simply slide right back down the back of your throat and get reswallowed. When *those* ones get sucked back up again, they're starting to get nice and moldy!

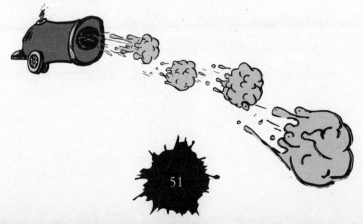

And you know when someone sniffs so hard and long that it seems like they are going to suck in the cat or the missing Lego piece from under the couch? Well, Jared and I have figured out that when someone does that ***humongous*** sniff, that's when the extra moldy boogers can be sucked from your stomach on to a super-highway straight up into your ears. As the boogers settle in, they get even staler, grosser, and more disgusting as they slowly turn into earwax. Every day they get thicker, cheesier, and greener until someone finally digs them out.

Jared always seems to have way more earwax than me and his is a sort of a dark browny-green color, while mine is a nicer lime green color. We each have our own jar that we keep by our bed at home and every night

before going to sleep we do another earwax extraction to add to our collection. The trick is to slowly slide your pinky finger in at the top and twist it around and down. That way the wax gathers on the tip of your finger and you get a nice big dollop that pops right out with a slight wiggle of your finger.

One time, Jared just shoved his middle finger straight in all the way to the knuckle and gave it a massive twist! He had so much earwax in there that the moment he twisted his finger the wax squelched all around it and created an airtight seal! Every time he tried to pull his finger out he thought he was going to drag his brains out with the wax! And the longer his finger was stuck in there, the more set the earwax got, and the more set the earwax was, the more painful it was when he tried to pull it out!

After an hour, his mother had to take him to hospital . . . I wasn't allowed to go, because I couldn't stop laughing! His mom wasn't impressed when the nurse called in another nurse for a look, who showed a doctor, who invited another doctor, who called in a specialist, who showed his students, who all scratched their heads until the hospital plumber walked by the door, saw the problem, pulled out his drain clearer grips, stepped into the room, grabbed Jared's finger, gave it a twist, and *POP!* Out it came!

The awesome thing was that the nurse then drained both of Jared's ears. He said they got a whole bucket of wax.

The bummer was that his mom wouldn't let him bring it home. ***Darn!***

But, every now and again we compare our earwax jars and check out how much we've collected. We use the wax to conduct some really interesting experiments.

Experiment 1: Consistency—We both take a good blob of earwax from our jar and hold it between the thumb and index finger—that's the one next to your thumb. We then slowly stretch our fingers wider and wider apart.

The moment the earwax splits into two parts we measure the gap between our thumb and finger. When he did it, Jared's fingers were only twelve millimeters apart, proving that his earwax is really thick and chunky. While the gap between my fingers was fifty-three millimeters! Obviously, my earwax is **waaay** stretchier than his!

Experiment 2: Texture—Next we take a good blob of *my* earwax and both of us smear it across our left cheek. Then we do the same across the right cheek with a blob of *Jared's* earwax. As we rub the earwax all over our cheeks we're able to compare the texture and graininess of the wax. We both agreed that Jared's earwax was definitely rougher and drier, while mine was smoother,

runnier, and definitely soaked into our skin more quickly.

Experiment 3: Taste—The taste test is definitely the worst experiment! If you've never tasted your own earwax, or someone else's, maybe you should! I double dog doo doo dare you to! It tastes kind of like that green wasabi stuff, or those red hot Mexican chilli peppers. And I don't mean that it's hot and spicy. I mean that you definitely don't want to go sticking your big fat finger into your ear, wiggling it about, yanking out a heap on the end of your finger, and shoving it in your mouth—unless you *reeeally* want to throw up! Just put a tiny bit of earwax on the tip of your finger and lightly touch it to your tongue.

Ewwwwwwwwwww! It's *so* bad! It's positively the worst, most disgusting, grossest taste ever! It's impossible to describe. But back to our quest to find out what we could use this stuff for. Once we each had a couple of small jars full of wax, well naturally the first thing we thought of was candles. If we could make candles with our earwax, then we could sell the idea to some big candle company and we'd be rich! The very first totally environmental, human candles!

We set to work right away by stealing a brand new box of Mom's little tea light candles. They're not your regular sized table candles; they're these small candles only about the size of a large coin, and about one and a half centimeters tall. They sit in a thin,

aluminum holder and only burn for about thirty minutes or so. Mom puts them all around the edge of the bathtub whenever she has a bath. She says that the candlelight and smell relaxes her. I think she just doesn't want to turn on the light and scare herself in the mirror!

We figured the little candleholders were the perfect sized containers to make our earwax candles in. Finally, after what seemed like endless years of fussing around, Mom headed into town to do the shopping. This was our chance. We zipped into the bathroom, grabbed her brand new box of fancy little candles, and yanked them out of the small aluminum containers. Then we threw the candles into the sink and began smashing them to *pieces* with the meat-masher hammer. As soon as we'd managed to get all of the wicks out, we turned on both taps full bore and washed all of the smashed up wax down the drain . . . We probably shouldn't have done that though, as the smell was so flowery and girly that it nearly made us want to throw up.

Next, we scraped every tiny little bit of ear wax from our jars into Mom's saucepan and turned on the stove to start heating it up. While the wax bubbled away we arranged the little containers in rows on the table, ready to fill. As soon as our earwax was melted we very carefully carried the pot across to the table where we poured the wax into the small containers, before poking the wicks into the hot liquid. Two hours later, they had set. It had worked perfectly! And the smell was definitely way better than the woozy, flowery version that Mom had. Our pot gave off an awesome, strong, manly smell. Like when you've been playing soccer all day long, in the middle of the desert in the hot sun, and you take your shirt off and shove your nose right in under the middle of your armpit and take a big long *snnnnniff!*

Beautiful! I was sure Mom would definitely love the smell of our candles way more than hers!

We decided to test just **how much more** Mom would love the smell by **not** telling her we replaced her candles. That way it would be a wonderful surprise and we could get her

61

honest reaction before we became rich by selling our candles to a candle company!

We carefully put our candles back in the original box and taped it closed.

That night I heard the familiar sound of the bath taps being turned on, just as I was getting ready for bed. I quickly shot Jared a message. This was it. We were on the brink of becoming millionaires, maybe even multimillionaires! I could hear Mom getting ready to have her weekly *"leave me alone I'm in the bath"* relaxation. I sat quietly in my room with Jared on the phone. We waited, listening for a sign. Finally, the taps turned off and the light shining around the edges of the doorframe flicked off. I could see the warm, dimly flickering light of the

candles below the door. Yes! She was using our candles!

There was the sound of water gently slooshing about as Mom submerged herself into the bathtub, followed by silence. Mom was obviously drifting away into her relaxation mode. I tiptoed down the hallway, sneaking closer to the door, and took in a huge breath. I could definitely smell the candles wafting through the gaps around the door. The smell was ***definitely*** manly! I raised an arm and took a deep ***whiff*** of my own armpit. Yep, same manly smell.

I could hear Mom sniffing over and over. Wow, she obviously couldn't get enough of the incredible scent.

I couldn't help but smile at our success

and was just about to text Jared with the awesome news when suddenly there was a heap of splashing, swearing, grunts, and groans coming from inside the bathroom. Weird.

"Are you OK Mom?" I called, wondering what was happening.

"OMG!" she yelled. "I paid a ridiculous amount of money for these candles! They're supposed to be relaxing, take away all of your stress, and make you feel as if you're floating on clouds. They're supposed to be made with some sort of incredibly rare flowers from the top of a mountain. They are supposed to smell like the flower gardens of heaven. ***What a load of crap!*** They smell like the disgustingly foul toilet bowls of a

soccer team on laxatives!" She was so angry! She went on and on while slipping and splashing about as she tried to get out of the bathtub as fast as possible—obviously trying to blow the candles out quickly before she threw up.

"I'm going to take these candles back to the shop and they are going to get a mouthful! Relaxing! They are making me feel . . . *bllluuurrr. Argh. @#%&!*"

Seems like just as Mom was getting out of the bath and her foot hit the floor, her guts exploded. Half her vomit spewed across the room, while the other half landed back in the bathwater. Her heel then slipped in the puddle of puke, making her fall backwards into the now vomit-filled bath, *splash!* The massive splash sent vomit and veggie bits slamming into the ceiling and bouncing off the walls, followed by a tidal wave that washed all of her own vomit right back over her face. Her spewy footprints from where she'd slipped, slid, and skated from the bath to the shower were all over the floor. And there was also a heap of chunky veggies and other gross stuff in the plughole that Mom would have to push through with her fingers to make it go down the drain. Oh yeah, and then there was vomit all over the walls, the ceiling, the mirror, the ornaments, and the towel racks. So, just a minor disaster.

Wow, the candle shop people were probably going to think Mom was totally crazy when she barged in there and

complained about the smell of their candles! Of course, if they actually lit the candles and smelled them they'd be running around like headless chickens trying to figure out what went wrong with that batch of candles. They might even need a bucket to throw up in too! Awesome!

Of course, I could tell Mom what really happened . . .

What! Are you crazy?

So Jared and I kind of figured that the candles idea was a bust . . . obviously girls don't smell things properly, because we thought the candles had an amazing smell.

I rubbed and rolled a blob of Jared's earwax between my fingers and thought about how much Mom had loved the smell—***not***! And then I had yet another brilliant idea . . .

PART TWO

Crabby Abbey was the snottiest girl in school and her birthday was coming up soon. Abbey is incredibly painful. She's like the biggest suck-up to the teachers of all time. They all think she's such a goodie goodie and believe absolutely everything she says.

Crabby could tell a teacher that pink alien cows had just landed in the playground and they'd believe her because "she would never lie"—yeah, right! Any chance she gets, she turns me or Jared in to a teacher for absolutely anything . . . even if she knows we didn't do it. Even if the "thing" hasn't actually happened yet! Even if it never was going to happen! "Mrs. Duckson, Sam and Jared stepped on some ants."

"Mrs. Duckson, half of Sam's foot touched the grass."

"Mrs. Duckson, Sam and Jared are breathing too loudly."

We thought that her birthday was the perfect time for some long overdue payback.

We'd noticed for a while that Crabby and her friends would go to the school bathroom about a hundred times a day. Every chance they got they strutted to the bathroom and came out five minutes later. Most times we didn't even hear a flush. Naturally, we figured there must be some sort of secret "Crabby Club." It was time to find out.

We spent days using our incredibly awesome spy-listening device behind the toilet block. It didn't take long to find out that it wasn't a club at all. Just some totally stupid "girly" thing where they check themselves in the mirror and put face cream on—about twenty times a day! Every time they went, we could hear Crabby droning on and on and on . . .

"My face cream is *so00* expensive. It comes from Antarctica."

"My face cream is made from the kisses of dolphins."

"My face cream is way better than the cream movie stars use."

She's such an exaggerator. She thinks that her face cream will help keep her looking beautiful and years younger when everyone else is in their seventies and she still looks twenty-one! Yeah, probably like a twenty-one-year-old warthog!

We were sitting around trying to come up with a new idea for how to make a million dollars from our earwax when Crabby wandered past, heading for the toilets with her nose in the air, face cream in her hand, and all of her little followers trotting along right behind her.

Face cream! We could use earwax to make face cream. We were going to be rich. Everyone would love it! It's natural—because it comes out of peoples' ears. It's good for you—unless you eat it. And it's cheap—because hey, it's earwax. And we could even try cat and dog earwax as well.

So Jared and I started experimenting to make it smell better, look better, and feel better! We added vinegar and salt and

Mom's favorite, really expensive perfume, as well as garlic, baked beans, lemons, brussel sprouts, and every other gross, disgusting thing we could think of. We thought if we put enough gross stuff together they'd cancel each other out and eventually make something awesome. Make sense!? We had our new formula, so all we needed to do now was try it out. And there was no way, no how that either one of us was going to put it anywhere near our own faces. Seemed like the perfect birthday present for Crabby Abbey.

Jared stole one of his mother's face creams, emptied it all out and replaced it with our batch. Then we carefully wrapped it up, ready for delivery.

We knew that Crabby was about to have some totally lame birthday party—she'd been going on and on about it for weeks. We heard about it every day at school. She kept boasting about how super amazing her party was going to be. She kept telling all of her dorky friends that she wasn't sure who she was going to invite so they'd all suck up to her in the hope of getting an invitation.

She said there was going to be a clown and a magician and horse rides and cotton candy and carnival rides and **blah, blah, blah**. Every time she walked past Jared and I, she'd look at us with an evil grin. We definitely knew that we weren't going to be invited and that was just fine by us! But of couse we would be **sooo** nice and give her a little present anyway. We just had to make sure that she didn't know who it was from, otherwise we'd be dead meat for sure. We had to find out the party details so that we could sneak in and slip her "present" in with all the others.

A few days later, we saw Crabby skipping around school and handing out fancy envelopes with her party invitations inside. We thought she put them in envelopes so that Jared and I wouldn't see them. *Ha!* Like that would stop us!

We waited until everyone was in class and then Jared asked if he could go to the toilet. I kept watch as he calmly walked out the door and slipped one of Crabby's invitations out of her bag as he walked by. As soon as he got the bathroom, Jared took out his cell phone, held the envelope up to the light, and took a picture. A copy of Crabby's invite—check! And with the details secure in Jared's phone, he simply returned the envelope to her bag on his way back to class. We were set to go.

That afternoon we confirmed the details of Crabby's party. All we had to do now was wait for Sunday.

We spent Saturday checking and double checking that everything was organized to execute our plan. There was only one thing left to do: ***Wrap the present so Crabby wouldn't be suspicious!*** If the wrapping paper wasn't just right, Crabby might realize something was up and start asking who the present was from. We sweated and swore,

folded and refolded, making sure we had nice sharp creases and even sides. We must have wrapped it at least a hundred times! The worst part was trying to tie a stupid pink ribbon around it. Now that was painful! But when it was finally done it looked perfect. It was a perfectly wrapped gift with a perfectly tied big pink bow on top.

First thing Sunday morning, I leaped out of bed, had breakfast, and headed over to Jared's place and triple checked our plan. "Let's go!" I yelled.

We jumped onto our bikes and rode over to Crabby's place making sure we would arrive about an hour before the party was due to start. We dropped our bikes in a ditch just down the road from her place and

covered them over with branches and bushes. We snuck from house to house with our gear carefully stored in our backpacks. Any time we thought someone might spring on us, we would dive over fences and hide in the bushes.

Crabby's house was just ahead. We snuck into her neighbor's yard and began dashing and creeping from spot to spot, getting closer and closer to Crabby's fence. By the time we'd finally reached our little hiding spot between the bushes and fence right next to Crabby's front room window, it was almost time for people to start arriving. We had to work fast. We carefully drilled a little spy hole in the fence to keep watch and waited. It wasn't long before everyone began to arrive and we started checking them off the list. We definitely didn't want someone turning up while we were "working."

As Crabby greeted each guest and they headed inside, we used our spy periscope to peek through the window to see where everyone was putting their presents.

80

It was so hard not to barf every time Crabby answered the door with her creepy, weird smile. She was being so sickly sweet— she does this thing where she pretends to be nice but she's actually being really mean. She was all like, "Oh it's *sooo* lovely to see you. Now don't worry that you've put on weight." "Wow, that's a pretty dress. Amazing that you can get such nice stuff from a second-hand store." "Thanks for the present. I'm glad you didn't get me much."

We watched as the presents were all placed on a big table in the living room across from the window that we were spying through— perfect! The presents were right next to a smaller table decorated with ribbons and glitter. That table held a huge, three-tiered, brightly colored birthday cake. It had a little ballet dancer on the top with her arms in the air and she was spinning on one toe. It was really fancy. But definitely lame! And of course, smack bang in the middle of the room was a big fancy camera on a tripod set up to capture the "fun."

Once everyone had turned up, they all headed out to the backyard for the party. As her parents closed the back door, Jared and I sprang into action. We were really getting into this spy stuff.

I took out my awesome, one-of-a-kind, way-cool, super sling-shot and took aim. *Twang!* I fired the special hook with a fishing line attached towards the window. *Whzzzzz!* It flew like a rocket, right on target . . . *smack*! Then we heard a *crack!* Oops! The window was closed and now it had a great big crack in it.

Jared dashed over and slid the window open. I fired again. *Twang!* It sailed through the window. *WhzzZZZ!* It caught the edge of a big canvas with a baby picture of Crabby Abbey in a pink ballet dress that was hanging right above the table with the presents. *Thwack!* Perfect! I attached our winder to the line while Jared popped our "present" into its special little holder and clipped it to the line. We had to move fast.

I began winding away to pull Crabby's special present along the line, as Jared kept watch through the periscope. If anyone walked in now we were dead for sure. I kept winding furiously. The package was swaying from side to side and moving faster and faster. In through the window it flew, winding and swaying. Across the hall, into the living room, winding and swaying. We were nearly there. A little bit more and . . . drop! I pulled the release pin and the package dropped right into the middle of the other presents just like we'd practiced.

"Crabby's mom is coming!" Jared whispered urgently.

I gave the rod a quick flick to release the catch-hook from the picture above the table but—**uh oh.** The hook was embedded in the canvas picture and the more I yanked the more stuck it became.

"She's at the backdoor!"

Ummm . . . I could . . . maybe . . .

"She's coming up the hallway!"

I yanked the hook like I had a whale on the end of my line and it worked! Sort of. ***Rrrrrrrip!*** The hook tore right down the center of Crabby's ballet picture, so it now looked like she'd been attacked by a ferocious, man-eating sabre-toothed tiger. I kept winding as fast as I could.

"Stop winding! She's at the living room door!" I stopped dead. The line was still laying on the floor across the middle of the room. We held our breath as Crabby's mother dashed across the room and stepped over my line without noticing. She grabbed something from a drawer and headed straight back outside. ***Phewww!***

"Go!" Jared whispered loudly. Once again, I wound like a madman and a few seconds later I just about had the line back through the window, when I hit a snag. Not again! *Tug tug tug! Tug tug tug! Twang whzzzzz!* Suddenly the line and hook came zooming back straight towards the center of my head at warp speed! I ducked. Jared didn't. *Eeeeeeee!* As I turned around Jared started whining. *Hmmm* maybe he was complaining about all the blood pouring out of his ear. Or the huge hook hanging from his earlobe. He actually looked pretty good with a fish hook hanging from his ear. It made him look kind of cool and tough. And I reckon the hook would be pretty handy too. You'd have somewhere to hang your keys.

I decided to have just one last look through the periscope before we took off. I probably shouldn't have.

I saw the torn picture drop and brush some of the flowers sitting in a vase at the back of the present table. Some petals gently floated towards Crabby's Xbox, past the sensor switch that turned on and popped open the disc tray. The disc tray smacked into one of the camera tripod legs, which sent the tripod and camera toppling over, straight into the middle of Crabby's birthday cake. *Splooshhh!* *Click, flash!* *Whzzzzz!* The camera snapped a picture. The stupid spinning ballerina on the top of the cake was sent rocketing through the air like a little ballet bullet until—*wack!*— she was embedded head first into the wall on the other side of the room. Her butt and legs were left sticking out of the wall—and were still spinning! It was time to run!

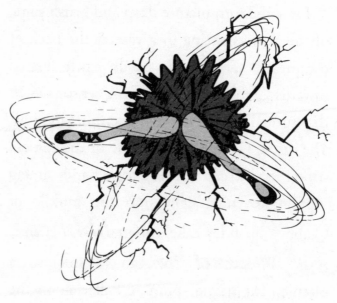

We shoved our gear into our backpacks and sprinted out of there as fast as we could —with blood still pumping out of Jared's ear

and his nice big fish hook earring dangling in the wind. When Jared got home he got into heaps of trouble for getting his ear pierced without his mom's permission. He spent an hour trying to explain to her that it was a fishing accident, but for some reason she didn't believe him!

For the first time ever, Jared and I couldn't wait to go to school the next day. We left nice and early so we could get there before Crabby Abbey. As soon as we got to school we threw our bikes and headed for the front gate. Toffee Thomas, Booger Boris, and all the other kids started to arrive. Finally, we saw her. Crabby was coming up the road. From a distance she looked pretty normal— for a crybaby suck-up. It was hard to tell if she'd used our cream or not. She was coming closer and closer.

When she reached the gates, she wandered through, pretending not to see us, as usual. We still couldn't tell if she'd used the cream. Although, she did appear to have a bunch of zits, and that was new.

We stayed out of sight and watched as Crabby's little band of followers started their daily suck-up routine of hovering, serving, and copying her. And then right on time— within the first five minutes of arriving at school—there she was off to the toilet to fix her face and reapply her face cream. Awesome!

We zipped behind the girls' bathroom and listened as Crabby started bragging about the wonderful new face cream she got for

her birthday that she was about to try! She was telling everyone that it was a mystery birthday present and she was sure it was from one of her rich aunties because it was so well wrapped! Jared and I high-fived.

On and on she blabbed, like she was a world expert on face cream. She was telling everyone that crushed diamonds were mixed through the cream and that the ingredients included teardrops from polar bear cubs, sieved through the wings of a very rare butterfly. (Okay, so I might be exaggerating a little). Then she added that she thought maybe the cream had been given to her by a secret admirer.

Secret admirer, what crap! I just about threw up on the spot. But we didn't care, as long as she kept rubbing plenty of our cream all over her face. It was the best day at school ever! Every time Crabby came out of the toilets she was so happy and her face was shining from the cream she'd just put on. But back in the classroom, Jared and I started to notice that Crabby's face was starting to tighten up and little cracks were showing, and getting wider every time she spoke. Of course, the tighter her face got, the quicker she ran off to the bathroom to put on more cream.

She was starting to look grey too. The worse things got, the faster she ran back to the bathroom to apply more cream. Around and around she went. It was hilarious to watch. By the end of the day, Crabby's face was the color of old moldy cheese and looked like smashed-up concrete. And the best part was she was **still** slathering on more and more cream to try and fix it!

Yep, try some of our "earwax face cream" today . . . it's great. Just ask Crabby Abbey!

TWISTED TALE: TERROR OF THE DEEP

"*Aarrrrhhhhh*, Melly look out!" I screamed as I shoved my little sister out of its deadly path.

Without any warning whatsoever, it appeared again. Every swimmer in the world would recognize the dark, evil shadow that sends a dagger of fear straight through your heart.

There was no time to think about whether putting myself in danger was the right thing to do or not, I just did it. But suddenly, without warning, it turned. "Help!" I yelled again, desperately hoping someone, anyone would hear my cries.

It was coming right at us!

Splash *splash* *splash*, *splash* *splash* *splash*

"Help!"

Splash splash splash, splash splash splash

We were in serious trouble! Why didn't we just stay out of the water!? I hated the water and everything in the water! Nothing good ever comes out of the water! Think about it. There are some of the most deadly, creepy animals in the world living in the water—most of them with rows of razor-like teeth just waiting to rip you apart. Crocodiles, sharks, killer whales, piranhas, and heaps of other vicious, weird creatures. Then there's all of those freaky looking jellyfish and sea snails and about a buzzillion other poisonous things that can kill you in minutes. And the ocean's

full of other totally gross stuff that people eat. Like mussels, snails, seaweed, and, *eewwwww,* oysters! Everyone knows what oysters *really* are! They're actually dolphin snot! Yes, really! Dolphins are really *really* smart so to get back at us for catching them and putting them in "marine parks" and making them do all of those embarrassing, lame little tricks like jumping through hoops, and waving and walking on their tails, they hide their boogers in empty seashells for us to find and eat. Gross! That's why dolphins are always making those weird "giggling" noises. They're laughing at *us* for eating *their* "booger oysters."

So why does anyone ever go into the water?! It's totally nuts!

Hey! I wonder whose job it was to go around tasting every weird looking thing a couple of thousand years ago?
You know, to see if stuff was "safe to eat" or "deadly poisonous"!
They must have found the dopiest people to do it!
I guess they quickly figured out that if the dope smiled ... then it was good.
If he smiled & threw up ... you cook it.
If he smiled & went green ... then cook it & add salt!
If he smiled, went green, & threw up ... don't bother cooking or eating it.
And if he smiled, went green, threw up, & died, then it was probably poisonous ... so cook it, add even more salt, & serve it to your annoying neighbors.

And now I had a reason to hate the water even more! I was trapped like a blowfly in steaming fresh camel poop. Stuck trying to save little Miss Smelly Melly, who could barely put her face underwater to blow bubbles. And now I had to save *her!?* I'm not that great at swimming. I was flat-out trying to save myself! Also, Melly's younger than me so she's not as useful. Mom hasn't had her for as long as me, so she hasn't had time to get as attached to Melly. She'd be able to forget her in no time!

I had tried to tell Mom before either of us even got anywhere near the water that it was far too dangerous. But does anyone ever listen to me? *NoOO!* "Off you go, and make sure you look after Melly," Mom had insisted. Oh yeah that's fair—*not!* Who did Mom think was going to look after *me!?* With one massive shove, I pushed her out of the way and Melly was safe again, for the moment! But there was no one to shove *me* out of the way. It was coming around again! With lightning speed, I reacted, diving

deep below the water's surface. There was nowhere to go but straight down. I knew there was no way that I could hold my breath underwater for any longer than even a minute! I dove as deep as I could go until finally my fingers grazed some slimey goop on the bottom. I was safe!

My lungs felt as if they were on fire as I used up the last bit of oxygen. But I had to stay under there for as long as I could. Every precious second gave me a better chance of survival, avoiding a fate that every swimmer fears and knows they're almost certain to come up against one day. I had to stay calm and not panic.

I couldn't believe this was really happening to me. All because I was stupidly trying

100

to save Melly, now I was a target as well! All because of my dopey baby sister! Why! Why did she have to be in the water with me?

I should've known this would happen. I'd heard horrible stories of others being attacked, in the same place, in the same way. I'd heard about their desperate cries of terror and their frantic screams. Now it was me that needed saving . . . and Melly, I guess.

One of my friends at school told me that his cousin, Dave, had been attacked. He was pretty lucky in one way though. He was in the water looking after his baby brother when the massive dark shadow appeared out of nowhere! The moment he saw it coming at them he let out a blood-curdling scream.

Dave was brave though. He definitely should have gotten a medal for bravery! He did everything he could to save his brother that day. And when it came back again, straight at them, Dave desperately tried to lift his brother out of the water, which meant he couldn't even use his own hands to defend himself. But seconds later, *bammm!* Dave twisted, screaming in agony as it brushed right by him, scraping along his side, leaving him scarred for life. He let out a massive horror movie scream and threw his body about wildly in fear.

Thankfully, his dad arrived just at that moment, and dragged them both out before it had a chance to turn back and attack them again.

Dave definitely saved his little brother, but he wasn't quite as lucky. The moment he looked down at his side the shock set in. Apparently, he never got over it and is now absolutely petrified of going anywhere near the water! He has terrible nightmares about it too, and wakes up screaming and thrashing about in bed most nights.

I had no idea how, but there was no way I was going to let that happen to me! No way!

But unfortunately, it seemed that no matter how loud I screamed, there was no one close enough to hear me. Where was everyone!? Did Mom just decide to wander off and let us take our chances? Did she just figure that I would save my whiny little sister if we got into trouble? I had no choice, it was all up to me!

With the weight of the water crushing down on me like some overweight elephant, my last few seconds of oxygen were running out fast!

I could feel my eyes bulging out of their sockets as if they were about to just **pop** right out and float to the surface and bob around like gloopy little ping-pong balls. My lungs burned as if I'd been sucking in fire all day long. The pain and agony got worse the longer I tried to hold my breath. I knew that I'd be forced to go back up for air any second now.

With a final push, my face suddenly broke free of the watery depths and I felt the warmth and light on my face again. Like a whale yawning on the surface, I stretched open my

mouth as wide as possible and sucked in the oxygen I'd been craving.

As I spluttered and splashed about, streams of water ran down my hair and rolled across my cheeks before spraying back into the water. Wiping the water away from my blurry

eyes, I slowly began to regain focus as I gasped for a second breath. Now, I was completely defenseless. My only hope was to get as far away as possible. I quickly began to scan the water's surface. I could almost hear my heart pounding. For a brief moment I thought I might actually have a chance. Maybe I'd be safe after all. Maybe it had turned away . . . but out of the corner of my eye I saw it. And it was coming!!

It was slipping through the water like some deadly torpedo, heading straight for me! Maybe it was actually intelligent! OMG! If it was smart enough to actually figure out which way I'd try to escape, there'd be no stopping it!

"Arghhh!"

I twisted suddenly and threw my body to the side just as it zoomed right past me. That was way too close. My heart was beating so loudly that I was sure it sounded like jungle drums. I quickly turned to see where Melly was when out of the corner of my eye I saw something, a shadow, a blur . . . could it be?

"Mooommm!" I yelled in desperation with the strength that I had left.

"Nooo!" It was coming back again. This time on a direct collision course! I knew that I didn't have the strength to keep on moving and trying to avoid it forever. There wasn't much time to think though. Soon it would be right on top of us. I had absolutely no idea what to do.

I tried to lie still on the bottom, all curled up to try and look as small as possible. My cheeks were puffed out like a couple of over-inflated beach balls as I desperately tried to make sure that I didn't release a single air-bubble that might give away where I was. Maybe it would just glide on over the top of me and keep on going. I was almost too scared to look up. Surely it had passed by now. As I cautiously pushed my face up towards the surface. OMG. It was still there!

And now I had an even bigger problem! My eyes were beginning to burn as if a hundred bees had rammed their great big butt-stingers straight into the center of my eyeballs. I had to move, but which way? And where was

Mom? Where was our rescue? I was doomed . . . and probably Melly as well.

I knew what I had to do. Melly was still bobbing about on top, to one side of me, and there was nice, clear water in the other direction. I knew I had to do the right thing.

Yep, I was going to save little Miss Smelly Melly Prissy-Pants from a fate worse than death. I was going to sacrifice myself to protect the little toad. I was going to take the hit for her. I would have to . . . Hang on. *Why* did I *have to*?

Melly was always going into *my* room, which she is definitely *not* allowed to do! And she's always taking *my* stuff, which she is definitely *not* allowed to do! She's always breaking *my* stuff, which totally sucks! And worst of all,

Mom always blames *me* because "You shouldn't leave your things laying around where Melly can get at them." **Blah blah blah**. "What if she swallows something and chokes?" **Yap yap yap**. Yeah, so that's fair . . . in another universe, that is! Melly is so annoying. She's basically a huge pain in the butt.

So why should I try and save *her* instead of *me*!?

That was it! I'd made up my mind.

I turned and slid along under the water moving towards Melly. My plan was to head straight at Melly full speed ahead! Straight towards her stomach. I knew our enemy would be following right behind me. Then at the very last second, I'd slip around behind Melly at the speed of light.

I figured it would be just like in those really awesome movies where everyone is shooting huge guns and firing deadly missiles at each other. You know, like when suddenly a missile is heading straight for the "goodie," who sees it coming and heads right for the "baddie" so that they'll both get splattered together. But then at the very last millisecond, the goodie dives out of the way and only the baddie gets blown to smithereens.

That's what I was going to do to Melly. Hopefully. I mean saving myself by using her as a human shield, not blow her up . . . well, unless it was absolutely necessary.

There was Melly, bobbing in the water, totally unaware that it was right behind me. I kicked one last time. Through my blurry

111

vision I saw Melly's face. Then, just as I was about to ram into her head-first, I swerved, rolled over onto my side and glided right by her, flipping over in one smooth move. I reached up, grabbed her by the shoulders, and shoved her right into its path. I desperately tried to propel myself as far away as possible, up and out of the water. I looked over at Melly, just in time to see the whole horrifying thing unfold right before my eyes.

Eeeewww, it got her! Right slap bang in her weird little belly-button. But she suddenly lashed out, punching at the water over and over, trying desperately to protect herself!

"Mom!" Melly screamed at the top of her lungs in her squeaky little girl's voice.

Slam!

Suddenly, Mom smashed the bathroom door back against the wall so hard that I thought the roof was about to crumble and fall in on top of us.

"Sam! Why didn't you lift Melly out of the bathtub when she had her little 'poop accident' in there . . . or at least try to keep it away from her? It's disgusting!" she said in her "I'm really annoyed" voice.

"But, but . . ." I stammered. "It's huge!"

"You used to have 'accidents' in the bathtub too Mister!"

"What?!"

"Right. You can wash Melly again after you've scooped her poop out of the bathtub and flushed it down the toilet!" Mom screeched.

"But, but . . ."

"Yes, I know it came from her butt, you don't have to keep reminding me!" Mom raged on. "Now for goodness sake, stop Melly splashing about and playing with it! And don't let her paint any more on her belly will you?!"

As I looked at the now water-logged, slimey poop sloshing back and forth in the bathtub and the poop-smeared Melly, my shoulders sagged.

Rats!

The Author

I remember my sister having an "accident in the bath" when she was a baby. Luckily, I wasn't in there at the time.

Happy reading!
Seeya,
S. B.

www.susanberran.com

Pssttt!

Hey ... want some more yucky gross stories?

Turn the page

Other books by Susan Berran

SNOT ROCKET

YUCKY, DISGUSTINGLY GROSS, ICKY SHORT STORIES

SUSAN BERRAN

?BARF BLAST

YUCKY, DISGUSTINGLY GROSS, ICKY SHORT STORIES

SUSAN BERRAN

120